The Cow in the House

A Viking Easy-to-Read Classic

retold by Harriet Ziefert
illustrated by Emily Bolam

VIKING

VIKING
Published by the Penguin Group
Penguin Books USA Inc., 375 Hudson Street, New York, New York 10014, U.S.A.
Penguin Books Ltd, 27 Wrights Lane, London W8 5TZ, England
Penguin Books Australia Ltd, Ringwood, Victoria, Australia
Penguin Books Canada Ltd, 10 Alcorn Avenue, Toronto, Ontario, Canada M4V 3B2
Penguin Books (N.Z.) Ltd, 182–190 Wairau Road, Auckland 10, New Zealand

Penguin Books Ltd, Registered Offices: Harmondsworth, Middlesex, England

First published in 1997 by Viking, a division of Penguin Books USA Inc.
Published simultaneously in Puffin Books

1 3 5 7 9 10 8 6 4 2

Text copyright © Harriet Ziefert, 1997
Illustrations copyright © Emily Bolam, 1997

LIBRARY OF CONGRESS CATALOGING-IN-PUBLICATION DATA
Ziefert, Harriet.
Cow in the house / by Harriet Ziefert ; illustrated by Emily Bolam.
p.   cm. — (A Viking easy-to-read classic)
Summary: Bothered by his noisy house, a man goes to a wise man for advice.
ISBN 0-670-86779-9
[1. Jews—Folklore. 2. Folklore.] I. Bolam, Emily, ill. II. Title.
III. Series.
PZ8.1.Z54Co 1997
398.2'089924—dc21 [E] 96-40057 CIP AC

Printed in U.S.A.
Set in Bookman

Reading level 1.9

The Cow in the House

Once upon a time,
a man lived in a
noisy old house.

CREAK!

The bed creaked.
The chair squeaked.
The roof leaked.

"This house is too noisy,"
said the man.

Drip
Drip

Squeak

The man went to town
to see a wise man.
"What should I do?" he asked.
"My house is too noisy.

The bed creaks.
The chair squeaks.
The roof leaks."

"Here's what you should do,"
said the wise man.
"Get a cow. And keep it in your house."

The man thought it was a silly idea.
But he said, "I'll do it."

The cow said, *Moo, moo!*
The bed creaked.
The chair squeaked.
The roof leaked.

drip

squeak

"My house is still too noisy,"
said the man.
"So get a donkey," said the wise man.
"And keep it in your house."

The man thought it was a very silly idea.
But he said, "I'll do it anyway."

The donkey said, *Hee-haw!*
The cow said, *Moo, moo!*

The bed creaked.
The chair squeaked.
The roof leaked.

"Now my house is even noisier,"
said the man.

"So get a sheep," said the wise man.
"And keep it in your house."

The man thought it was a stupid idea.
But he said, "I'll do it anyway."

The sheep said, *Baa, baa!*
The donkey said, *Hee-haw!*
The cow said, *Moo, moo!*

The bed creaked.
The chair squeaked.
The roof leaked.

"I can't live in my house!"
said the man.

"So get a cat," said the wise man.
"And a dog, too!"

Another dumb idea, thought the man.
But he did it anyway.

The dog said, *Woof, woof!*
The cat said, *Meeow, meeow!*
The sheep said, *Baa, baa!*
The donkey said, *Hee-haw!*
The cow said, *Moo, moo!*

The bed creaked.
The chair squeaked.
The roof leaked.

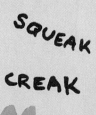

Now the man was mad.
Very mad!
He yelled at the wise man.
"I told you my house was too noisy!
You told me to get animals.
Noisy, noisy animals!
I am going crazy
from the noises they make!"

The wise man waved his arms.
"Do what I tell you!" he shouted.
"Put the dog out of the house!
Put the cat out of the house!
And the sheep!
And the donkey!
And the cow!
Put them all out!"

BAA BAA

So the man put them all outside.

He went back inside and got into bed.

The bed creaked.
The chair squeaked.
The roof leaked.

Drip

squeak

"Oh, what a quiet house!"
said the man.